For Jake, the Worthi to my Nelli

Tiny Troubles: Nelli's Purpose
Copyright © 2024 by Sophie Diao
All rights reserved. Manufactured in Italy.
No part of this book may be used or reproduced in any manner whatsoever without written permission
except in the case of brief quotations embodied in critical articles and reviews. For information address
HarperCollins Children's Books, a division of HarperCollins Publishers, 195 Broadway, New York, NY 10007.
www.harpercollinschildrens.com

ISBN 978-0-06-321446-0

The illustrations for this book were created digitally.
Typography by Caitlin E. D. Stamper
24 25 26 27 28   RTLO   10 9 8 7 6 5 4 3 2 1
First Edition

Tiny Troubles

Nelli's Purpose

written and illustrated by
Sophie Diao

HARPER
An Imprint of HarperCollinsPublishers

Don't forget to stay hydrated!

Feeling better, Nelli?

Uh-huh.
But I still want to know where my purpose is.

Are you sure it isn't this snail?

Yes, I'm pretty sure.